The Case
of the
Perfect
Prank

Read all the Jigsaw Jones Mysteries

And Don't Miss . . .

Coming Soon . . .

The Case
of the
Perfect
Prank

by James Preller
illustrated by Jamie Smith
cover illustration by R. W. Alley

A
LITTLE APPLE
PAPERBACK

SCHOLASTIC INC.
New York   Toronto   London   Auckland   Sydney
Mexico City   New Delhi   Hong Kong   Buenos Aires

ISBN 0-439-55996-0

12 11 10 9 8 7 6 5 4 3 2 1   4 5 6 7 8 9/0

Printed in the U.S.A.   40
First printing, April 2004

For Gavin, my pal. Boo!

—JP

CONTENTS

Chapter One

Polar Bears in Winter

When I first opened the box, all I could see was white. Snow and ice and frozen wind. Slowly, shapes began to form. A polar bear moved toward me, followed by an Arctic fox.

Yet I was not afraid.

After all, I was safe in my bedroom. Wearing shorts and a T-shirt. Trying to finish a brand-new jigsaw puzzle.

That's when Joey Pignattano knocked on my bedroom door.

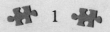

"Hi, Jigsaw. What are you doing?" Joey asked.

"An impossible jigsaw puzzle," I replied, showing him the cover of the box. "It's called 'Arctic Winter.'"

"It looks like spilled milk to me," Joey said. "Everything's white."

"Not if you look closely," I said. "That's the thing with jigsaw puzzles. If you work on them long enough, you start to see little details."

"It would make my head hurt," Joey concluded. He plopped down on the edge of my bed and sighed loudly. I turned to look at him. Joey wore glasses and, judging by the bird's nest on top of his head, he didn't own a comb. Another thing about Joey: He liked to eat — anytime, anywhere, anything. Even worms and broccoli. But that didn't matter. Joey was one of the nicest kids in Ms. Gleason's class. Today he seemed like a guitar with a broken string. A little out of tune.

"You got any new cases?" he asked me hopefully.

I shook my head. "Business is slower than a thick milk shake."

"Too bad," Joey said, frowning. "You remember how I helped you out on that case a while ago?"

I remembered. Disasters, after all, are hard to forget. My partner, Mila Yeh, had been busy, so I asked Joey to put a tail on Bigs

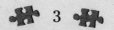
3

Maloney. Instead of following Bigs, Joey taped a cottontail to the big lug's butt. Yeesh.

"I was thinking that maybe I could work with you and Mila," Joey offered.

"I don't know, Joey," I said. "We're sort of doing OK without you."

"Yeah, I know, I stink anyway," Joey mumbled unhappily.

"You don't stink, Joey. It's just that, um,

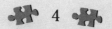

you don't have a lot of experience," I told him.

Joey's eyes brightened. "You could teach me, Jigsaw! I'd even work for free," he said. "It's not about the money. I just want to be a detective like you."

A voice in my head warned, *NO, NO, NO!*

I should have listened to it. "Follow me, Joey," I said, rising to my feet. "Let's test your detective skills."

Chapter Two

The Test

I sat Joey down on our living room couch. "Wait here," I told him. "I have to get some things."

A few minutes later I came back with a bucket. I placed some objects on the table in front of Joey. You know, the usual stuff: Spider-Man action figure, puzzle piece, cookie, baseball card, fork, marble, television clicker, and so on. Finally, I took out an egg timer.

"You're gonna cook some eggs?!" Joey asked hopefully.

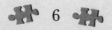

I laughed. "No, Joey. This isn't about eating. That's one test I'm sure you'd pass. I want to test your observation skills."

"My . . . what?" Joey asked.

"A good detective must be able to look closely at things," I explained. "That's how we find clues and solve mysteries. For this game, I want you to study the objects on the table. Try to remember everything you see." I turned over the egg timer. "You've got thirty seconds."

When time was up, I covered the objects with a towel. I asked, "What do you remember?" Once again, I turned over the egg timer.

Joey blinked in concentration. "A fork . . . a puzzle piece . . . and . . . um . . ."

"Hurry, Joey," I said. "Time is running out."

"A COOKIE!" he exclaimed. "It was chocolate chip. Homemade, I figure. A little burnt on one side. Still, it looked kind of moist, the way I like 'em."

"OK, OK, enough about the cookie," I said. "What *else* was on the table?"

Joey confessed, "To tell you the truth, Jigsaw, once I saw the cookie, it was hard to look at anything else." He shrugged, then asked, "Can I eat it?"

"No, you can't eat it!" I exclaimed. "Let's try this." I took the towel off the objects. I asked Joey to observe closely. Then I told him to look away. That's when I removed the marble and the fork and added a spoon.

"What's different?" I asked him.

"Um . . . let's see," Joey said, pondering deeply. "The cookie is still there, that's good."

And so it went. When it came to spotting small details, Joey was hopeless. Except when it came to cookies.

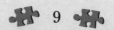

Just then, my brothers Daniel and Nicholas slinked toward the kitchen, giggling to themselves.

"What are you guys up to?" I wondered.

"You'll see tomorrow morning," Daniel said with a sly smile. "Just remember to wear your raincoat."

Hmmm. Sounded fishy to me.

Daniel and Nick had a new goal in life. They wanted to be exactly like the Weasley twins from the Harry Potter books. If there was trouble to be found, they found it. And if they didn't find it, they created it themselves.

After they left, I turned back to Joey. "Can you believe those two . . . ?" But then I noticed that something was missing.

I eyed the objects on the table.

The cookie had disappeared.

I glanced at Joey. Chocolate lips. Crumbs on his lap. Happy as a bee on a buttercup.

You don't have to be a detective to solve some mysteries.

Chapter Three

April Fools!

The next morning, I awoke to screams.

"AAAACK!"

I leaped out of bed with my dog, Rags, at my heels and followed the sound of the screams.

I saw my mother at the kitchen sink.

Her shirt and face were soaking wet.

And she didn't look happy.

Daniel and Nick were bent over laughing, pointing, and shouting, "April Fools!"

Somehow my oldest brother, Billy, and my thirteen-year-old sister, Hillary, slept

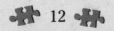

through the whole thing. Teenagers are gifted that way.

My mother stood still, slowly dripping. My dad tossed her a dish towel. "They got you again, huh?"

My mother glared at Daniel and Nick. Slowly the corners of her lips lifted. And she smiled. "Every April Fools' Day," she said. "The same trick every year. When will I ever learn?"

Daniel and Nick looked at my dad and high-fived with delight.

The trick was an oldie but a goodie. At our house, we have one of those sinks with a spray nozzle. You squeeze it, and water comes out of the nozzle instead of the faucet. The trick is to tie a rubber band around the nozzle. Then you aim the nozzle outward. Daniel and Nick must have done it last night, when they were giggling in the kitchen. Come morning, my mom went into the kitchen to make her "necessary" pot of coffee. She just turned on the water and . . .

. . . splash, the spray hit her!

It works every time.

This didn't give me an easy feeling.

First, Daniel and Nick got my mom. I knew that I was also on their list. I might as well have had a bull's-eye on my back. It was only a matter of time. Because when it came to April Fools, Daniel and Nick didn't play favorites. Everybody was a target.

The Weasley twins would have been proud.

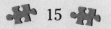

Chapter Four

The Shower

I invited Ralphie Jordan and Mila over that afternoon to play Clue.

Luckily, Ralphie was the first to arrive. I told him about the practical joke my brothers had pulled. He loved it. Then I pulled out a whoopee cushion. "I borrowed this from Nick," I explained.

The doorbell rang again. I could see through the curtains that it was Mila. "Watch this," I said. I took the whoopee cushion and hid it under a couch pillow.

Mila had been my partner for years. She was my best friend in the world. But on April Fools' Day, anything goes.

Noise screeched from the basement.

"Oh my gosh," exclaimed Mila. "It sounds like a cat is caught in the washing machine."

"Nah," I explained. "That's just Daniel and Nick playing their new electric guitars. They say they want to start a new rock band called Doctor Pain and the Toothaches."

Ralphie laughed.

Mila rolled her eyes.

After a pause, I patted the pillow on the couch. "Sit down, Mila. I have to tell you something important."

I winked at Ralphie. Mila sat.

Pppoooofffttt!

A loud noise filled the air.

Mila's eyes widened. Her face went red with embarrassment. She shot up, looked at the seat, and picked up the whoopee cushion.

Ralphie and I just laughed and laughed.

Mila scowled. She looked mad.

"Ha-ha," Ralphie bellowed. "April Fools, Mila! The joke's on you!"

"Very funny," Mila groaned.

"Aw, come on, Mila," I complained. "You just can't take a joke."

Mila looked at me, then at Ralphie. She pulled on her long black hair. Then she

smiled, sort of. "You're right," she stated. "Maybe I'm too sensitive. I guess it was pretty funny."

We played Clue for a while, then my mom made lunch for everybody. Grilled cheese and grape juice. What more could a detective ask for? My dad didn't eat with us. Instead, he wandered around the house, scratching his head and muttering, "A hammer, a hammer. My kingdom for a hammer!"

Go figure.

Later that afternoon, I took a shower.

In my clothes.

It happened like this: Ralphie, Mila, and I were drawing pictures in my room. I went into the kitchen to get some Pringles. When I got back, they were gone.

"Um, guys?"

"We're in here," Ralphie called from down the hall. "In your brothers' room."

"You've got to come see this," Mila said. "Hurry!"

So I hurried.

When I pushed open the door, I felt Niagara Falls come down on my head. Then I heard the howling laughter of four voices followed by a chorus of "April Fools!" It was Mila, Ralphie, Nick, and Daniel.

I looked up. Somehow they had rigged a

bucket on top of the door. It was tied to a string. When I opened the door, it tilted and poured the water out.

Those guys were sneaky.

I felt the water soak through my shirt and slowly run down to my socks.

"Got any soap?" I asked.

Chapter Five
The Client

On Monday afternoon, April 2, at exactly 4:26 p.m., Mila and I sat in my tree house and watched Danika Starling push a dollar bill into my money jar.

I wrote in my detective journal:

THE CASE OF THE KIDNAPPED CAT

I had to admit, it had a nice ring to it.

My client, Danika, sat with her legs crossed. Her braids fell down on both sides of her face. The beads in her hair clicked when she moved. Danika kept looking at Mila, then back to me. She seemed nervous.

"Let me see that note again," Mila asked.

Danika handed Mila the sheet of paper. The note was neatly typed. It was one of the strangest things I'd ever read.

> April showers bring bad news. I've stolen your cat. And that's that. No joke.
>
> Fools may try, but they can't fool me. So don't even think about getting *Fou-Fou* back.
>
> Revenge is mine!
>
> Signed,
> The Practical Thief

"Where did you find this note?" I asked Danika.

"It was in my mailbox," she replied.

"That's odd," I said. "Do you usually —"

Mila interrupted me with a question. "Who could have possibly done this, Jigsaw?"

"A thief always leaves clues," I calmly stated. "There is no such thing as the perfect crime. We've just got to look at this case piece by piece . . ."

". . . like a jigsaw puzzle," Mila said.

"That's right," I commented. "Just like a jigsaw puzzle."

"When did you first notice that, er" — I checked my notes — "Fou-Fou was missing?"

"When I woke up," Danika quickly replied. "Let's see. It was, like, seven in the morning. Usually Fou-Fou sleeps in my, like, room. She's so cute and cuddly and, like, everything. And, um . . ." Danika hesitated. She looked at Mila's face.

"You said that you usually give Fou-Fou a

bowl of milk in the morning," Mila said helpfully. She glanced at me and explained, "Danika told me about the case in school today."

I doodled absentmindedly in my notebook. When I looked at it, I realized that I had drawn a picture of a cat.

"Fou-Fou," I murmured. "What kind of name is that?"

"It's just . . . a name . . . I guess," Danika said sheepishly.

"Rags was already taken," Mila joked.

"Yeah," I chuckled. "I suppose Fou-Fou is an OK name . . . for a cat. Do you have a photograph?" I asked Danika.

Danika looked at me blankly. "A photograph?"

"Yes, Danika," Mila said. "I'm sure you

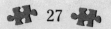 27

have a photograph. *At home*. Maybe you can give it to us," she prodded. "Tomorrow."

Danika nodded and smiled. "Sure, sure, I can get you a photograph, no problem."

"Describe the cat to me," I said.

Danika's eyes flickered. "Um, let's see. She's Siamese. Very beautiful. You know how they look — brown with green eyes, pretty black markings on her head and tail."

After a pause, she asked, "Can I go home now?"

"I have a few more questions," I said.

"You do seem upset, Danika," Mila said soothingly. "You must be very worried. It's probably a good idea for you to go home and rest. Don't you think so, Jigsaw?"

I didn't think so, exactly. But I didn't say so, either. "I guess the questions can wait until tomorrow. We'll need to look at the scene of the crime," I told Danika.

Danika said that after school tomorrow

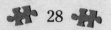

would be fine. Then she climbed down from the tree house and hustled out of my backyard in record time.

"Strange," I murmured.

Mila read the note again. "Yes, it sure is strange. It's creepy to think that there's a cat-napper out there somewhere."

I cleared my throat. "You're right, Mila. But when I said 'strange,' I was thinking about Danika. She's acting weird."

April showers bring bad news. I've stolen your cat. And that's...

Mila shrugged. "She's just upset. It's got to be hard to lose a pet."

"Yeah, I guess so," I agreed. "The funny thing is, before today I didn't know that Danika had a cat!"

"Some detective you are." Mila laughed.

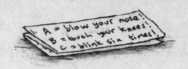

Chapter Six

Joey's Code

Tuesday morning was clear skies and smooth sailing. So I rode my bike to school with my brother Nick, who is a fifth-grader. We got there a few minutes before the buses arrived. We locked our bikes and went inside.

My teacher, Ms. Gleason, usually chats in the hallway while we slowly fill the classroom. I was sitting on the reading rug when Joey came up to me. "I've been practicing being a detective," he whispered. "I even figured out a great new code."

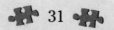

"Cool," I said. "Show me."

"Outside during recess," Joey said. "I need plenty of room to move around."

I raised my eyebrows but decided not to ask. With Joey, it's best not to ask questions. The answers are too strange.

Mila sprawled on the rug beside me. She jabbed me in the ribs as a greeting. "Danika says to come over at four-thirty," she said.

I frowned. "Why not right after school?"

Mila shrugged. "Beats me. Anyway, it works out better this way. I'll go home first to practice the piano."

During recess, Joey explained his new code. I sat on the tire swing and listened.

He began, "You know how there's that code where the number one is really the letter A, and number two is the letter B, and number three is the letter —"

"Yeah, yeah," I interrupted, not wanting to hear him go through the entire alphabet.

"It's called a substitution code. You use numbers instead of letters to spell out words. It's the simplest code in the detective handbook."

"Well, I was watching a baseball game on ESPN last night. They showed the third-base coach giving signals to the batter, and I got an idea," Joey said.

He handed me a piece of paper. I glanced at the top of it.

A = blow your nose!
B = touch your knees!
C = blink six times!
D = scratch your armpits like a monkey!

"Looks hard," I said doubtfully.
"No, it's really easy!" Joey exclaimed.

"Watch. I'm going to tell you to meet me at the tree house after school in my new supersecret code." He winked.

I sat back and watched in amazement.

Joey leaped around, scratched, sneezed, and did jumping jacks. He tugged on his socks, combed his hair, twirled around in circles, picked his nose, and hopped up and down.

Then he started to pant and turn red in the face. He paused. "This is making me tired," Joey complained.

"I'm getting tired just watching you," I joked. "Nice try, Joey. But while you may be *trying* to tell me to go to the tree house after school, it LOOKS like you are a ballerina who just got stung by a bee."

"You don't like it?" he asked, still winded.

"It's okay," I lied. "Maybe I'll try it someday."

I saw the disappointment in his eyes.

"I stink," he moaned.

"What are you doing after school?" I suddenly asked.

"Nothing," Joey replied.

"Maybe you can help me out on a case," I offered. "What do you think?"

The big smile on Joey's face gave me all the answer I needed.

Things couldn't go too badly, I figured. As long as Joey didn't try any secret codes.

Chapter Seven

Stops Along the Way

I had asked Joey to meet me at my house after school. The plan was for my oldest brother, Billy, to give us a ride to the new pet store in town. It's called Fur, Fins, and Feathers.

Billy frowned when I asked him. "I'd love to help you out, pal," he said, "but I've got people to do and things to see."

"Er, you mean things to do and people to see," I corrected.

"Whatever!" Billy laughed. "The bottom line is, I can't help you out."

Oh, well, we had to ride our bikes instead. If we hurried, there would still be enough time to make it back to Danika's by four-thirty. Unfortunately, Joey made us stop at the candy store. Once inside, he stood at the counter, just looking at the candy. After a few minutes, I nudged Joey and asked, "Well? Aren't you going to buy anything?"

"Nope."

"Nope?"

"No money," Joey explained.

"Then what are we *doing* here?" I asked.

"I just like to look," Joey said, rubbing his belly, "and dream."

Yeesh.

I knew the owner of Fur, Fins, and Feathers. His name was Jax. I helped him out on a case a while back. He always called me Little Holmes, after the great detective Sherlock Holmes. But Jigsaw was good enough for me. Besides, Sherlock Holmes was make-believe. He was a guy you'd read about in books. Not like me. I was real.

And today, I was real *late*.

So I hustled toward the counter — past fish tanks and birdcages, Gila monsters and rabbits.

Joey stopped to poke his finger into a Siamese cat's cage.

"Come on, Joey," I called. "We don't have time for that."

At the sound of my voice, Jax looked up from the counter and smiled happily. "Little Holmes, my main man of all men!" he exclaimed. "What gives?"

Jax didn't talk like most people. And that's probably a good thing. Otherwise, everybody in the world would be pretty confused. Jax was really nice and everything. But kind of . . . different. He was the kind of person my Grams would call a "hippy-dippy flower-power type."

I got right to the point. I introduced Jax to Joey and asked, "Do you know anything about any cat-nappings?"

Jax's eyes widened in surprise. "Meow, dude! A cat burglar? Does this mean you're on another case, detective?"

I nodded.

Jax stroked his long mustache. "Can't say I've heard anything about cat-napped kitties," he mused. Then Jax took a bite of something that looked like a stick.

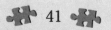

"Granola?" he offered.

"No, thanks," I politely refused. (I had tasted granola once before and that was more than enough for me.)

Joey, of course, reached for it happily. He chewed slowly. And slowly, his smile turned to a look of surprise, then sadness. "It tastes like tree bark," he complained.

Jax laughed. "You have to get used to it, little dude. This is nature's feast. Lots of fiber. Good for the old plumbing, if you know what I mean."

We didn't know what he meant, and we hoped to keep it that way.

"Funny you should come in today, Little Holmes," Jax began. "A couple of friends of yours came in for a visit not fifteen minutes ago —"

CRASH, BANG!

A cat toy display crashed to the floor. Suddenly, a ferret and a cat ran around the store. Jax liked to give his pets "space to be free." A parrot squawked, "Big noise! Big noise!" *SQUAWK! SQUAWK!*

Jax scrambled behind the counter, knocking over magazines and granola bars. "Crazy critters," he laughed. "They keep me hopping!" He bent to pick up the display.

"Er, we gotta go," I told him. "But if you hear anything about stolen cats, let me know."

"Sure thing, Little Holmes!" he answered cheerfully. "Catch ya on the rebound."

"Yeah, sure, on the rebound," I echoed. Then I whispered to Joey as we walked out the door, "Whatever that means."

Joey and I climbed on our bikes and headed home. Joey had to get back to his house.

Me? I had to visit the scene of a crime. I had some questions for Danika that still needed answers.

Chapter Eight

Puzzling

I was twenty minutes late. Mila was waiting outside Danika's house when I arrived.

She was humming to herself. I knew the tune and remembered the words:

"Little bunny fou-fou,
Hopping through the forest,
Scooping up the field mice,
And bopping them on the head."

"You're late," Mila noted.

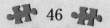

"Joey," I complained. "I've seen turtles pedal faster."

I was about to tell her that I'd been to Jax's store when Danika opened the front door. She placed a finger over her lips, whispering, "My mom is resting upstairs. Let's be quiet. And Jigsaw," she added, "please don't mention the cat-napping to my mom. She's very upset about it."

We followed Danika into her den. It was a small room with a large television set and a comfortable couch. "Here's the photo of Fou-Fou," Danika said, handing me a Polaroid. It was taken with one of those instant cameras that spits out the photo while you wait. The picture showed Danika hugging an unhappy-looking Fou-Fou. It wasn't the best photo in the world. It was a little blurry and dark, but it was good enough.

"This cat looks kind of familiar," I mused. "I feel like I've seen it before."

"You probably have," Danika said. "Fou-Fou is always wandering around."

"*Nooo,*" I murmured. "That's not it."

"All Siamese cats look alike," Mila observed. "If you've seen one, you've seen them all."

I leafed through the pages of my detective journal. "You said you found the note in your mailbox," I recalled.

Danika nodded yes.

"And that was on Sunday, right?"

"Yes," Danika quickly replied. "I like to check the mail. I've got a birthday coming up, and I was hoping for a card from my aunt Zaza — she always sends me money," Danika explained. "That's when I found the note."

"Some birthday present," I said.

Mila smiled, watching Danika intently. Mila was usually full of questions, but today she didn't seem to have any.

"So you think Fou-Fou was taken while she was outside," I said.

Danika nodded. "Yes, I'm sure of it. Mila and I think she was cat-napped when she was wandering around in the neighborhood."

"Sounds reasonable to me. My dog, Rags,

 49

was once taken by a girl who wanted a pet," I told Danika. "So I know you must feel crummy."

"Oh, yes!" Danika purred. "It's just awful."

I glanced at Mila. If Danika felt awful, she hid her feelings well. Maybe *too* well.

"It's strange that the cat-napper left a note," I said.

"Really?" Mila asked.

"Well, think about it, Mila." I ticked off the reasons on my fingers. "First, the cat-napper has to take the cat. Second, he or she has to bring the cat somewhere. Then the cat-napper has to come all the way back to leave a note. I mean, why bother? It doesn't make sense."

Mila rocked back and forth, thinking it over. "I guess it *is* odd," she finally agreed.

"Can I see your room?" I asked Danika.

"Well, sure," Danika said, standing up. "Why?"

"Fou-Fou slept in there with you, right?"

Danika's lips tightened. "Yes, yes, all the time."

Danika's room wasn't what I expected. It wasn't all pink and flowery and full of dolls. She had Rollerblades dumped in one corner, a hockey stick, and soccer posters on the walls. "That's Mia Hamm," Danika explained. "The best woman soccer player ever."

Danika's bed was made. The pillows were fluffed and tidily placed.

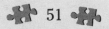

"Hmmm," I frowned. "No cat fur?"

"What?"

I grinned. "When Rags sleeps with me, there's fur all over the place."

Mila spoke up. "Siamese cats don't shed very much, do they, Danika?"

"That's right," Danika said. "And I think my mom just changed the sheets."

A few minutes later, we headed out the door. Mrs. Starling met us at the bottom of the stairs.

"Oh, hello, Jigsaw, Mila," she greeted us warmly. "Are you leaving so soon?"

We told her we were. "Don't worry about Fou-Fou, Mrs. Starling," I added. "We'll get to the bottom of this. You can count on Jigsaw Jones, private eye."

Mrs. Starling didn't say a word. She just stood with her mouth open.

Mila tugged hard on my arm. "Let's go, Jigsaw. NOW!"

Chapter Nine

Putting the Pieces Together

"What's the big hurry?" I asked Mila when we got outside.

"Danika said that her mom was upset," Mila explained. "She *told* you not to mention Fou-Fou."

"Her mom looked OK to me. Besides, I was just trying to make Mrs. Starling feel better," I answered.

Mila was on foot, so I walked my bicycle beside her. "This case just doesn't add up," I said. "I wonder if Danika is telling us the whole truth and nothing but the truth."

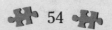

Mila stopped in her tracks. "Not telling the truth? Why would you think that?"

"The mail," I answered. "Everybody knows mail is not delivered on Sundays. It seems strange that Danika would check the mailbox on a Sunday afternoon."

Mila shrugged. "Just lucky, I guess."

I didn't answer. Instead, my brain raced with a hundred thoughts. Did something else happen to Fou-Fou? Was it somehow Danika's fault? Why did the cat-napper

write *Revenge is mine*? Revenge for what? Could the note have been a fake? I asked Mila if I could see the note when we got to her house.

"Did you notice anything strange about it?" I asked her.

Mila shook her head. "It seems like a standard cat burglar note to me."

"You haven't been a lot of help, detective," I joked. "I might have to replace you with my new helper, Joey Pignattano."

"Good luck!" Mila laughed. Then she added kindly, "I'm sure you'll figure it out, Jigsaw. You always do."

When I need to think, I do jigsaw puzzles. So that night I pulled out the "Arctic Winter" puzzle again and brought it to the living room.

My sister, Hillary, sat moaning and groaning on the couch. No, Hillary wasn't sick from some rare tropical disease. She had something far worse. Homework.

Hillary was studying for a French test, and she was not one to suffer in silence. Between pitiful moans and painful groans, Hillary repeated French vocabulary words out loud.

I pushed aside the puzzle and studied the note once more. I had a feeling that I was missing something. Maybe the note held a clue and I just couldn't see what it was. Maybe my detective skills were slipping.

April showers bring bad news. I've stolen your cat. And that's that. No joke.

Fools may try, but they can't fool me. So don't even think about getting *Fou-Fou* back.

Revenge is mine!

Signed,

The Practical Thief

The Practical Thief, I thought. *That's just plain weird.* I took a big swig of grape juice.

That's when I remembered where I had seen Danika's cat before. At Jax's pet store! But . . . it couldn't be, could it? Joey had stopped to poke his finger into the cage. A Siamese cat was in there. It looked exactly like Fou-Fou. Could Jax be the cat-napper? Could the cat-napper have sold Fou-Fou to Jax?

Meanwhile, Hillary kept reciting French words in the background. It was getting on my nerves. I was about to ask Hillary to please stuff a sock in it, when she said something that stopped me cold.

"Wait!" I exclaimed. "What did you just say?"

"Huh?"

"Did you say Fou?" I asked Hillary.

Hillary groaned. "Yeah, *fou.* It means 'fool' in French."

I reread the note. Fou-Fou. It wasn't

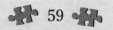

a name. It was a clue. A clue left by a very clever person. "*Fools may try...*" I read again. "*April showers... no joke... Revenge.*"

I scribbled a list of important words in my journal. And there it was:

April   Fou-Fou
joke   Revenge
Fools   Practical

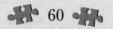

I moved the words around, trying to put them together like puzzle pieces. *Practical . . . joke*. Then I saw the clue I had been missing all along. The first words in each of the three paragraphs.

How could I have been so blind?

Danika Starling didn't even own a cat!

Chapter Ten
The Last Laugh

Looking at it now, it was all so easy. Finished puzzles never look very hard. Yet when all the pieces are spread out on a table, well, it's a different story.

Of course I didn't realize that Danika had a cat . . . because she didn't. But what about the photo? Then I remembered. It was taken by an instant camera.

I thought back to my visit to Fur, Fins, and Feathers. What was it Jax had said?

"*A couple of friends of yours came in for a visit not fifteen minutes ago . . .*"

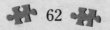

Then the display fell, and Jax never finished his sentence.

It was Mila and Danika. Taking a photo . . . of a Siamese cat!

I circled the three key words in the note. Mila had sent me a secret message. She was testing my detective skills the whole time.

April.

Fools.

Revenge.

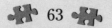

Mila didn't like it when I tricked her with the whoopee cushion. Then she decided to get back at me with a practical joke of her own. The answer to the mystery was in the note all along. It was the perfect prank!

Then I remembered the song Mila had been humming. Mila didn't hum "Little Bunny Fou-Fou" by accident. She was giving me another clue. That's where she got the name for Danika's phony cat!

I raced out the door and ran down the block to Mila's doorstep.

"Jigsaw!" she exclaimed.

(She was wearing footsie pajamas.)

"You got me," I admitted.

Mila smirked and scratched her head. "I don't understand," she said.

"I think you do," I replied. "Do the words 'April Fools Revenge' mean anything to you?"

Mila couldn't help but laugh. "You figured it out!" she said proudly.

"With a little help from Joey . . . and a lot of help from you," I replied.

"I gave you enough hints," Mila said, beaming. "But you have to give credit to Danika. I knew I needed somebody to help me with the practical joke. Danika did a great acting job."

"So there never was a Fou-Fou," I concluded.

Mila shook her head. "No Fou-Fou," she replied.

"Good," I said. "It's a stinky name. Even for a cat!"

I turned to leave. "Well, good job, Mila. You got your revenge. I guess I deserved it. But there's one last thing."

Mila raised her eyebrows. "Oh? What's that?"

"I'm keeping the dollar," I said. "This is one job we don't split fifty-fifty."

Mila smiled. "It was worth every penny!"

About the Author

James Preller often draws upon his own life as a basis for his Jigsaw Jones books. Like Jigsaw, James Preller has a slobbering, sock-eating dog. Like Jigsaw, James was the youngest in a large family. His older brothers called him Worm and worse — yeesh! And so do Jigsaw's!

James and Jigsaw both love jigsaw puzzles, baseball, grape juice, and mysteries! But even though Jigsaw and James have so much in common, they are not the same person.

Unlike Jigsaw, James Preller is the author of more than 80 books for children, including *The Big Book of Picture-Book Authors & Illustrators; Wake Me in Spring; Hiccups for Elephant;* and *Cardinal & Sunflower.* He lives outside of Albany, New York, in a town called Glenmont, with his wife, Lisa, three kids — Nicholas, Gavin, and Maggie — his cat, Blue, and his dog, Seamus.

Here's a sneak peek at the next

A JIGSAW JONES MYSTERY®

#24 The Case of the Glow-in-the-Dark Ghost

*J*igsaw and Mila are always ready to take on a new case. Unless it means looking for clues in a haunted school!

This new mystery has them searching school buses, spying on classmates, and dusting for fingerprints in the school cafeteria. Yuck! Will the hunt for clues help Jigsaw and Mila solve this spooky mystery? Or will they just end up in the principal's office?

Jigsaw and his partner, Mila, know that mysteries are like jigsaw puzzles—you've got to look at all the pieces to solve the case!

____	0-590-69125-2	#1: The Case of Hermie the Missing Hamster	$3.99 US
____	0-590-69126-0	#2: The Case of the Christmas Snowman	$3.99 US
____	0-590-69127-9	#3: The Case of the Secret Valentine	$3.99 US
____	0-590-69129-5	#4: The Case of the Spooky Sleepover	$3.99 US
____	0-439-08083-5	#5: The Case of the Stolen Baseball Cards	$3.99 US
____	0-439-08094-0	#6: The Case of the Mummy Mystery	$3.99 US
____	0-439-11426-8	#7: The Case of the Runaway Dog	$3.99 US
____	0-439-11427-6	#8: The Case of the Great Sled Race	$3.99 US
____	0-439-11428-4	#9: The Case of the Stinky Science Project	$3.99 US
____	0-439-11429-2	#10: The Case of the Ghostwriter	$3.99 US
____	0-439-18473-8	#11: The Case of the Marshmallow Monster	$3.99 US
____	0-439-18474-6	#12: The Case of the Class Clown	$3.99 US
____	0-439-18476-2	#13: The Case of the Detective in Disguise	$3.99 US
____	0-439-18477-0	#14: The Case of the Bicycle Bandit	$3.99 US
____	0-439-30637-X	#15: The Case of the Haunted Scarecrow	$3.99 US
____	0-439-30638-8	#16: The Case of the Sneaker Sneak	$3.99 US
____	0-439-30639-6	#17: The Case of the Disappearing Dinosaur	$3.99 US
____	0-439-30640-X	#18: The Case of the Bear Scare	$3.99 US
____	0-439-42628-6	#19: The Case of the Golden Key	$3.99 US
____	0-439-42630-8	#20: The Race Against Time	$3.99 US
____	0-439-42631-6	#21: The Case of the Rainy Day Mystery	$3.99 US
____	0-439-55995-2	#22: The Case of the Best Pet Ever	$3.99 US
____	0-439-55996-0	#23: The Case of the Perfect Prank	$3.99 US

Super Specials

____	0-439-30931-X	#1: The Case of the Buried Treasure	$3.99 US
____	0-439-42629-4	#2: The Case of the Million-Dollar Mystery	$3.99 US
____	0-439-55997-9	#3: The Case of the Missing Falcon	$3.99 US

JJBKLST0504